CARDS OF LOVE

THE HANGED MAN

CLARISSA WILD

Copyright © 2018 Clarissa Wild
All rights reserved.
ISBN: 978-1723869174

This is a work of fiction. Names, characters, places and incidents are either the product of the author's imagination or are used fictitiously. Any resemblance to actual events, places, organizations, or person, whether living or dead, is entirely coincidental.

All rights reserved. No part of this book may be reproduced, transmitted in any form or by any means, electronic or mechanical, including photocopying, recording, or by any information storage retrieval system. Doing so would break licensing and copyright laws.

MUSIC

PLAYLIST

"Heaven" by Majical Cloudz
"Can't Pretend" by Tom Odell
"Jealous Sea" by Meg Myers
"I Can't Go On" by Kaleo
"Everybody Knows" by Sigrid
"The Way Home" by Sleep Dealer
"I Run To You" by Missio
"Westworld - Main Title Theme" by Ramin Djawadi
"Stadium Pow Wow" by A Tribe Called Red
"The Animals" by The House of the Rising Sun

PROLOGUE

Lillian

After

It's finally time.

I grab one of the dull pencils from the tray and a piece of paper from the stack and place it down in front of me. Biting my lip, I stare wistfully at the sheet, wondering what I should write. If I should even write anything.

There are so many things I want to say, so much I have to explain, but none of the words in my head will suffice. She'll never understand. She's too innocent to know the truth.

So I opt for something else instead. Something familiar

and loving, so she'll know how much I care.

"Are you gonna start or what?" the woman across the shoddy table says while glaring at me.

I look up from my paper and gaze blankly ahead. "As soon as I know what to write."

"You don't get much time, y'know," she adds, shrugging. "Suit yourself."

I nod a few times. Advice is best not taken for granted, so I pick up the pencil and rub my lips together.

Dear Daisy,

You'll probably never read this letter, but I want you to know that at least I tried. I've told your auntie Dana to hold onto the letters I send her until I get the chance to hand them to you myself. As much as I want to, I can't be with you right now. But I promise it won't be long. I'll be with you again soon. Before you even know it.

I know you'll be good. I know you'll do great out there in the world.

And you know … I will find you again.

Love,
Mommy

Smiling, I read over the words again before my letter and those of all the other women next to me are taken by the guard as she passes us.

They'll read the contents and decide whether it's suitable to send.

This is how it always goes … here in prison.

There's no choice to make, no autonomy whatsoever. Nothing but sleep, eat, work, and wait.

Wait until your time is up.

Until you can see your baby again.

But I knew the consequence when I did what I did. That I'd end up sacrificing precious time I could've spent with her. But it was the only choice I could make, and I'd do it again in a heartbeat if I had to.

It's no one's fault. Not mine or his.

Circumstances brought me here, and I accept that wholeheartedly.

Love … is what brought me here.

I made the ultimate sacrifice for my little girl.

For a man I couldn't stop loving even when that same love ripped her away from me.

For both … I'd willingly hang.

***

HANSON

I park my green truck on the side of the road near the long, dry grass. Another truck is approaching not far up ahead, so I step out of the vehicle and shut my door. Tapping the top, I silently wait until it stops right in front of mine. The sun blocks the view as the guy steps out, but I can still make out a smile.

"And?"

"It worked," Brandon says as he whisks an envelope from his back pocket. "You were right."

"They wouldn't follow you from her sister's place," I say as he walks toward me.

"I didn't even see her. She just left a key on her porch and sent me to a PO box to get this." He holds it out to me.

As I reach out to grasp the envelope, he maintains his hold, looking me straight in the eyes. "I'm doing this for you because I'm your friend, but—"

"I know," I say, nodding. "I know what she sacrificed."

"Good," he says, licking his lips. Then he releases the envelope and turns around.

"Thanks," I say as he walks back to his truck.

All I get is a quick glance and a hand going up in the air before he climbs back inside and drives off. But it's enough to know our friendship is still alive, even after everything that happened recently.

Besides, I have other things to worry about now. There's a whole world out there begging me to explore it.

It's what she would've wanted me to do.

I bear the burden now to live a fulfilled and happy life because I owe it to her. To the woman who gave me my freedom back … in exchange for her own imprisonment.

ONE

HANSON

Present

I run through the thick fog, zigzagging through the woods, avoiding stumps and rocks as best as I can. I trained for this all these months, so I have to give it my all. I have nothing to lose.

Nothing will stop me from reaching my goal … Freedom.

I know I don't deserve it, but damn, did I hunger for it.

And now I'm finally out here in the real world again.

This was unplanned and completely outrageous. I didn't think I'd succeed, but now I don't want to stop. The more I run, the bigger the grin on my face even though I know it's wrong. The farther away I get, the bigger the taste for more. The outside world is waiting for me.

Despite my brain telling me to go back, to surrender, to fight this selfish desire, I can't stop myself from putting one foot in front of the other and doing everything I can to stay out of their claws.

Even when I'm being chased and forced to run and swim for miles on end, I can't give up.

The primal need inside me is too strong to ignore.

I *must* escape.

I *have* to see her.

***

Lillian

A few weeks later

The onions are strong, but they're not making me cry. Maybe because I refuse to ever cry, not even for the onions. There's only one exception … *her*.

I chop the onions into tiny pieces. They smell good today. Perfect for the pasta I'm making with homemade tomato basil sauce. A vegetarian dish with a sprinkle of parmesan cheese. Daisy's favorite.

I never used to like cooking much, but I do it with love

for her. Especially when she gives me that sparkly eyed look when she peeks into the pot to see what I'm making. She grins and squeals. "Pasta! Yay!"

"Go set the table, honey," I say, smiling back at her.

She tiptoes around the kitchen, trying to open the cabinets that are just out of reach, so I give her a hand by lifting her. "There you go."

Her face is radiant as she grabs the plates and carries them to the table, so proud of every little thing she can do to help. It's as though she's catching up on every little thing she missed. It's sweet, and it definitely reminds me of myself, always wanting to be a little more grown up than I was. Boy, do I miss those days with no work, no drama, and no bills to pay.

I sigh and dice the garlic before adding it to the sauce while Daisy places the utensils and two glasses on the table. She runs back into the kitchen and washes her hands under the sink, but as she runs away, she forgets to turn off the faucet.

"Daisy! You left the water running," I call out.

She doesn't reply.

Then the screen slams shut.

I place down my knife and gaze outside when I notice her running through the grass. My eyes narrow. She's chasing something … a paper plane.

My heart begins to palpitate.

There shouldn't be a paper airplane here.

We live on a farm in the middle of nowhere. My nearest

neighbor lives miles away.

Shit.

I drop everything and run after her, but as I exit the house, I stop dead in my tracks. A man in the distance captures my attention; his short black hair in stark contrast with the bright afternoon sun. The look on his square face dead serious as he stands there, his feet firmly planted on the soil.

Only his eyes follow her …

"Daisy!" My voice is primal. Like the call of a lioness whose cub is in danger.

"Look! A paper plane!" Daisy holds it up in the sky like some kind of trophy.

I want to rip it from her hands and shred it to pieces. Burn it to the ground. But I can't take my eyes off her and neither can he.

"Come here, Daisy," I say with a stern voice. It's harsh enough to make the smile disappear from her face.

She comes to me slowly, but when she's within arm's reach, I grab her tight and hold her close to my body. I cling to her as if he could take her away at any moment. Maybe he could. Would he?

The mere thought makes the hairs on the back of my neck stand up.

"Go inside," I say, still glaring at the man standing on my property.

I can't let him get any closer. I have to stand my ground.

However, the moment I release Daisy, and my eyes

briefly follow her inside, he's already taken five steps forward.

"Stop," I say.

I'm not afraid. I'm not afraid.

I repeat that mantra over and over in my head—as if hearing it often enough will make me believe it—but my knees are buckling with each step he takes.

"Hi …" His voice is rough but smooth. Like a stone in a river sanded down by time.

What is he doing here? Stalking us?

"I just wanted to see you," he says, taking a step toward me.

"Stay away," I say, inching back.

I'm shaking like a leaf. I don't want him to see, so I straighten my back and ball my fists, burying my nails in my skin.

The closer he gets, the weaker my knees feel, so I follow my instinct and grab my cell phone. I don't think as I dial 911 and show him that I mean business.

"You don't have to do that," he says, holding up his hand.

"Yes, I do," I bark, and I turn around and run back into the house. As the door slams shut, a woman picks up on the other end. "Hello, yes? I need the police."

The woman asks for the reason, so I tell her a man on my property is refusing to leave. I'm in full panic mode now, running solely on adrenaline as I lock the door and close the windows.

However, as I look outside at the rustling high grass, I lower my phone.

He's gone.

TWO

Lillian

When the police arrive, he's long gone. My heart has calmed down, but my mind hasn't. And as the police officer approaches the door, my entire body feels constricted. As if I can't breathe or move a limb.

"Hello, ma'am." The police officer tips his hat. "You called for an intruder on your property?"

I nod, but I don't feel like I'm even here. I feel as though I'm there off in the distance … with him.

I wonder where he went. If he'll try to come back.

If I'd be able to resist when he does.

"Ma'am?" the police officer repeats.

"Um … yes, I did," I mutter, trying to pull myself back together. "It was a homeless man, I think. But he's gone now." I clear my throat as the man narrows his eyes at me. He must think I'm losing my shit. A homeless man in the middle of nowhere? Yeah, right.

"You're sure he's gone?" he asks, cocking his head to peek inside. He's probably trying to find out if I'm being forced to say that. Or maybe if I'm being held at gunpoint.

I wish I had that excuse. How pitiful.

"Yeah," I reply casually as if it's nothing.

"Ma'am, is there anything else I can do?" he asks, still eyeing me as if I'm hiding something. Or maybe he truly thinks I'm being held hostage.

"It's fine. I'm fine. He's gone. We're fine." I open the door. "See?"

He gazes around. "All right," he says, nodding.

"Sorry I called," I add. "I was a bit panicky, but we're good now."

"Don't you worry about that, ma'am. We've got you covered." He winks as he turns around. "But it'd better not be a prank call."

"No, no," I say, laughing it off like it's no big deal even when it is.

As he walks off, the little voice inside my head wants to tell him to stop and turn around, but I don't. Not until he's gotten back into his car and driven off do I feel like I can breathe again.

I shut my eyes and let out a sigh, closing the door.

I don't know why I didn't tell that police officer the truth.

Maybe a part of me still believes there's a possibility …

No.

I can't ever think like that. Ever.

I turn around and immediately shriek. Daisy's right in front of me. "Don't sneak up on me like that, honey," I say, breathing out a sigh of relief.

"Sorry," she replies. "Who was that man?"

"A police officer," I answer, smiling as I bend over. "He was just checking on us."

"No, I mean the other man, Mommy."

I blink a couple of times. My feet are frozen to the ground.

I swallow away the lump in my throat and look through the window, wondering if we'll ever see him again. "No one, honey. No one at all."

***

HANSON

"Next," the cashier says, and I put down the sandwich, a newspaper, and a card.

It's one with little purple stars on them and a pink moon, and on the inside, it makes a sound when it's opened.

It's expensive but worth every penny.

"That'll be seven thirty."

I fish some coins out of my pocket and place them down. There goes all my money. Well, not all of it, but it still feels like an arm and a leg for the sandwich, a newspaper, and a card. I don't make much these days. Not with my reputation. I gotta do the odd jobs—the random delivery jobs where you don't even know what you're carrying around—but they pay, so I do it. Gotta earn a living somehow.

The cashier snatches away my money as he looks at me with contempt.

They always do. *They* being everyone who's not native.

I don't mind it anymore because I'm used to it. I ignore them like they ignore me. It's best that way.

I grab my stuff and am walking toward the exit when I notice an older woman with her hair tied in a knot and a strange yellow scarf staring at a newspaper. She turns her head, and our eyes lock. She blinks her eyes a couple of times, and then her face turns white as if she's seen a ghost. One glance at the newspaper is all I need.

Fuck.

I rush out of the store, pulling up my zipper to hide at least my mouth inside my jacket. It's not much, but it'll have to do. I should buy a cap and sunglasses ... and maybe a wig too.

I didn't think they'd still be running my story after all this time, but I guess an escape never goes unnoticed. I don't have any plans to get caught, though, so I quickly get inside my truck and slam the door shut, then start the engine.

One thing's for sure, though; that woman recognized my face from that photo.

Here's to hoping I won't ever see her again because I'm pretty sure she's going to call the cops.

I gotta be careful, especially around these parts, and *especially* after she called the cops on me at the farm. She surprised me with that one. Then again ... of course that's what she'd do, knowing what I did.

My soul is stained, and I live with the consequences every day. I can't ever forget that even though I'd like to sometimes. You never know who's your friend and who's your foe when you're someone like me.

A fugitive who's escaped prison.

So after throwing a final dirty glance at the old lady still staring me down from inside the store, I hit the gas and drive off. Another place I can cross off my list as safe.

***

Lillian

The light of the moon guides me across my yard to the barn. I slide open the wooden doors and walk inside on bare feet. The hay feels warm under my toes as I turn on the small light to my left, illuminating the barn.

In the middle on a bale of hay sits a man.

It's *him*. In the flesh. *And* he's completely naked.

I try to swallow, but my throat feels clamped shut. Still, my heart can't help flutter.

"You came," he says, lifting himself up. He stands tall. Proud. Wide-legged. Unafraid to show what he's got to offer, and boy, is it a lot.

Jesus. My mind is trailing off fast.

My eyes try to avoid the dick dangling between his legs, but it's difficult not to look as he's approaching me. Hard not to look at his hard-on.

"I've waited so long," he says, his voice sultry, thick with desire.

I lick my lips at the sight of his rippling muscles and v-line as he traps me against the wooden door. I hold my breath as he leans in and takes a whiff of my scent. His musky, testosterone-laden smell fills my nostrils and makes me feel dizzy with lust.

God, what I wouldn't give for that man to touch me. To

have a taste and not feel guilty.

A coarse hand slides through my hair and down my neck to my chest. He's barely avoiding my breasts as if he's tempted but not quite convinced he should.

"I missed you," he says, and an arrogant smile follows.

Three words that completely undo me.

My lips part, but I can't get the words out of my mouth. I don't know what to say, so I opt for nothing at all. His smile is infectious even when it shouldn't be.

He shouldn't be here. We shouldn't do this. It's wrong. Forbidden.

Yet I need to. I must.

After all this time, I need to know.

So when he leans in to plant his lips on mine, I don't back away. I don't fight him off. I let him kiss me. I let him touch me, grab me by the waist, and shove me against the door. The wood pokes my skin just like his length as he nudges up against me, making me feel how badly he wants me.

I can hear it in his groans.

Feel it in the way he gropes my ass.

Licks my tongue.

Fuck. Me.

Suddenly, my eyes burst open, and I'm no longer in the old barn under the dirty light. I'm in my bed with my sheets completely soaked.

And my clit is thumping.

Fuck.

Now I feel even filthier than I felt in my dreams.

The morning sun greets me, reminding me of my duty. My reality.

I sigh and throw the blankets off, yawning with annoyance. Time to take a really long cold shower.

THREE

Lillian

While Daisy holds the cart in place, I open the back of the car and load the groceries inside. It's way too hot to stay out this long, and we still need to bake the cookies for her school project tomorrow, so I have no time to waste. Plus, she still needs her meds, and I left them back at home, so we're in a hurry.

However, Daisy wants to bring the cart back on her own, which I promised her she could do last time, so I guess we'll take a bit longer today. She wants to grow up so fast. I wish I could explain to her how wonderful it is to be young. You lose that part of your life so quickly, and it's always after the fact that you realize how much fun it was not to have to worry about anything.

Still, I have to be careful not to spoil her. That tends to happen often with single moms, they say. Especially with girls as fragile as she is ...

Images of her lying on a cold, hard bed while relying on machines come to mind. The tears still sting my eyes when I think of the nights I spent bawling at her side. I quickly brush them away. She's doing so well these days.

I smile as she rolls the cart away with a grin on her face. It seems to go fine, so I quickly turn around to close the trunk. However, when I turn around to look for her again, she's standing still near the collection of carts ... talking with a man.

It's him.

"Daisy!" I yell.

But she doesn't turn; she doesn't even seem to notice me. She can't hear me all the way across the parking lot.

I rush toward them, not giving a shit that my car is still unlocked.

He's leaning over, handing her something. I can't see what it is except that it's wrapped in a newspaper. It could be anything—something dangerous for all I know—so I snatch it out of her hands and throw it aside, then drag her away with me. I don't say a word to him.

He was about to hand her a card as well. I don't know what it said, and I'm not interested in it either. I just want to get as far away from here as fast as possible.

To think she almost ... *no*, I refuse to let my mind go there. "What did I say about taking things from strangers?" I hiss.

"Strangers?" she mutters, gaping at me with her big brown eyes. "But Mommy, he—"

"No," I repeat, grasping her hand. "We're leaving."

"Wait!" she says, and she manages to rip away from me.

She hastily fishes the newspaper package from the ground and runs back toward me, but not before throwing a wistful glance at him. All I can do is stare and fume.

I'm lucky she returns to me. Still, it doesn't put me at ease. Not even a little bit. Not with him around. What is he doing here? How does he know where we are? Why can't he leave us alone?

"Lillian!" His voice breaks every train of thought I have.

I turn and shout, "Leave us alone!"

He follows us all the way back to my car. "I just wanna talk."

"There's nothing to talk about," I reply as I swiftly push Daisy into the car. "Sit down, honey, and don't get out."

"Please, you have to give me a chance to explain," he says, still trying to come closer.

"Don't," I say, holding up one finger.

For some reason, this makes him stop. That, or my unapologetic glare. I probably look murderous. That's because I am.

"What are you even doing here?" I ask, my voice breaking. "Can't you just leave us be?"

The desperation must be visible because he stops trying to approach, which gives me enough time to get into the front seat and ram my keys into the ignition. I don't even look as I drive off, knowing he's still there. Vigilant. Watching over us.

"Who was that man, Mommy?" she asks.

I don't reply. I don't know how to answer that question.

"He was at our home too, wasn't he?"

"Mmmhmm …" I mutter.

A crackling noise makes me look through my rearview mirror. She's unwrapping the newspaper. I'd completely forgotten about it. Fuck.

"Throw that away, please," I say with a stern voice. It could be a weapon for all I know. Whatever it is, it can't be good.

"No," she says with a soft voice, almost as if she's about to cry.

I gaze through the mirror again. My eyes widen.

It's a plush toy. A stuffed blue penguin.

"Can I keep it?" she asks, her eyes lighting up. "Please?"

For a second there, all I wanna do is scream and shout. *No. No. No!*

But I don't.

It'd make her unhappy, and I don't ever want to see her unhappy. She deserves every ounce of lighthearted fun in her life. And if this toy is what she wants, how can I say no?

"All right, all right," I say with a lopsided smile.

"Yay!" She hugs the toy tight. "Thanks, Mommy!"

"And promise me you won't ever talk to strangers like that again," I add, cocking my head at her.

"I promise," she says, still snuggling with the soft penguin. "But Mommy …"

The way her voice chirps up at the end makes goose bumps scatter on my skin.

I already know what she's going to say, but it doesn't make it any less hard to take.

"That man … He wasn't a stranger, was he?"

***

HANSON

I wish I could've given her more than merely a stuffed toy.

With a sigh, I stare at the car as it disappears down the street.

For a second there, I thought about chasing them. But that wouldn't be right even though it takes every ounce of self-control not to do exactly that.

I sit on the bench in front of the supermarket and stare at the card in my hand, wondering when I should try again. If I even should. I know she probably won't read it. She'll most likely throw it out into the trash right away.

I would too if I knew it came from me.

She's frightened of me. Anyone would be if they knew what I've done. If they'd seen the choice I made.

Still, it broke me to see the fear in her eyes. All I want to do is give them both what they deserve.

But I guess it'll have to wait until next time.

***

Before

The gun is shaking in my hand.

"Please, don't!" the guy says.

"Shut up!" I yell back.

I try not to tremble, but I can't stop my muscles from reacting to the adrenaline. Can't stop my lungs from breathing out ragged breaths. Can't stop my lips from quaking as I speak.

"Don't say another word," I say. My voice is fluctuating in tone, but I remain steadfast in my position … with the gun pointed straight at his head.

"Please, there has to be another way," the man says.

There isn't. This *is* the only way.

I've thought of all the other options. All the possible ways this could've gone. This was the sole choice I could make.

But he wouldn't understand. No one ever would.

Even though the curtains in this shitty hospital room are closed, sunlight still peeks through and momentarily blinds me. He tries to take a step toward me, so I scream, "Stop!"

I don't have time to waste. The longer I wait, the higher the chance guards will intervene. I can't let it happen.

"Please, don't do this," the man utters, grasping the metal bed behind him that he's shackled to.

I move my thumb to the safety and push it.

His pants turn a different shade of blue. He's pissed himself. I guess any man would.

For a second there, I almost lower my gun, but then I stop myself midway. I pitied him when I shouldn't. He doesn't deserve the empathy.

This is where it gets tricky because I know that if I do this, I'm just like him.

I become what I hate the most. A criminal.

But knowing what he did, there isn't a chance in hell I can let him live.

"Everyone will hear you shoot me," he says.

I shake my head. "Not a chance. This thing's got a silencer."

"Please, I beg you. Let me go." He's getting desperate now. "I'm still going to die anyway, but it'll be long and painful instead," the man says, bawling his eyes out. It's like he's trying to come up with reasons he should live. As if you can call being a vile creature like him *living*.

He clasps his hands together. Mucus drips from his nose and mouth. He looks pathetic like that. I wonder if people will look the same at me when I'm done with him.

"I know you think you need to do this, but there are

other ways to punish me. I'm already going to jail for a long time. Nothing's worse than that for someone like me. What else do you want?"

Someone like *him*.

He means old men who touch little girls.

Even in prison, they're the most hated scum on the planet.

"You deserve this," I say, holding the gun against his head. I'm doing the world a favor.

"No, no, no, please!" he begs, still gazing at me as if it will change my mind.

Nothing ever will.

Not with this.

I made up my mind a long time ago. When I knew what was at stake.

But for her … I'll gladly become a murderer.

Bang.

FOUR

Lillian

Present

I grab the bottle of pills I placed on the nightstand and take two of them out. Then I grab the glass of water and hold them in front of her. "There you go."

Daisy sighs. "Do I really have to take those?"

I raise a brow and cock my head. Really? She's going to try this again? "Yes, and you know why."

"I know," she says, swallowing. "But they taste nasty."

"I'm sorry, honey. I would make them taste better if I could, but I can't. Tell you what, pinch your nose closed while you swallow. Then it won't be as bad."

She frowns but grabs the pills nonetheless. "Fine."

She takes the glass of water from my hand too and chugs down the pills. Pinching her nose, she clenches her eyes shut as if she's having trouble downing them. Still, the thirst-quenching sound she makes when she's done tells me it wasn't quite as bad.

"Done!" She hands back the glass with glowing eyes.

"Good job." I run my fingers through her hair and press a kiss to her cheeks. Then I grab her teddy bear and tuck it under the sheets with her. "Time to sleep."

"Wait. Where's Mr. Puddlewuddle?"

I narrow my eyes. "Excuse me, who?"

"The blue penguin I got!" She folds her arms. "Did you throw him away?"

"No, of course not, honey," I say. For a second there, I wish I had. But then she'd probably hate me.

"I want him to be here too," she says, putting all her effort into her pout.

"All right, I'll take him out of your drawer," I say, rolling my eyes as I fetch the stuffed animal.

"Yay!" she squeals, clapping her hands. She pulls away the sheets and pats the bed. "Mr. Puddlewuddle can sleep right here next to me."

There's a slight pang in my stomach, but I ignore it as I place the toy where she wants it. I don't understand how she can get so attached to something she's had for just a day. Then again, children often do when they feel like something's missing.

I let out a sigh and kiss her again on the forehead this time as I tuck her in. "Sleep tight, honey."

"Wait," she says again as I'm about to leave. "What about the card that was in the mailbox?"

I pause, clenching the doorframe. My lungs feel constricted.

She knows. She saw it. A smile creeps onto my lips. Of course, she did.

I'd hoped I was good at hiding things, but apparently, I'm not.

"It was for me, wasn't it?" she asks. I'm surprised she noticed. "Can I read it?"

"No," I bark. I don't know why I'm being so resolute. So mean. Maybe I'm jealous of her ability to see him as anything but dangerous.

"Sorry, honey," I say, glancing over my shoulder, trying to be milder. "Maybe another time."

"Tomorrow?" she asks as I'm about to close the door.

I close my eyes and let out a final sigh. "Maybe. Ask me again tomorrow."

***

I lie awake in bed for hours.

This is how it always goes. How it's been for years.

I don't want to use the sleeping pills that I got from the doctor because then it feels like defeat, and I don't like to give in to defeat. But they're staring at me from my nightstand. If I don't take them, I don't get enough sleep. And being a cranky bitch to your child isn't really all that either. So after a few more minutes of simmering in my own stew of self-hatred, I grab the bottle anyway.

Right as I open the bottle and throw two pills onto my hand, I hear some noise. I put the pills back and place the bottle down, then get out of bed. I quickly check on my baby girl to make sure she's all right. That's when I hear the noise again.

It's metallic. Like someone's messing with the door lock. And it's coming from downstairs.

In my pajamas, I make my way downstairs, clutching the bannister. The noise gets louder and louder, so I hurry to the closet in the hallway and grab my shotgun. It's the only protection I have, and boy am I glad I bought the damn thing.

I snatch the box with ammo from the shelf and open it with trembling hands, trying not to panic. I've only done this twice, but I manage to put the bullets in properly before I move closer to the door. The noise has stopped, and no one is messing with the front door, at least not that I can see. Did I imagine it? Or maybe it's the shoddy door and just needs to be replaced. I mean, it *is* windy outside.

Still, I gotta make sure, so I turn the lock and push open the door. Shivering, I take a step outside and look around, holding the shotgun tight.

Suddenly, something moves in the corner of my eye, and I immediately point my shotgun at it.

"Who's there? Show yourself!" I yell.

A figure steps out into the light that shines right underneath my porch.

There's no mistaking it. The old leather jacket. The square, chiseled, scruffy jawline and penetrating eyes.

It's *him*.

"Hello."

His voice makes my skin tingle and not in just a good way—in an oh-my-God-I'm-losing-my-panties way. But I can't let him get to me so easily.

"What are you doing here?" I ask.

His hand opens up, showing me a key. So it was him trying to open the door. "You forgot this one. Better not try to hide keys under the windowsill."

"I replaced the locks," I hiss, burying my feet into the ground.

"No wonder it didn't work," he says. "Good."

Why would he even say that?

And why do I immediately think of that dream I had?

"Tell me why you came," I say with a bold voice, remembering my defiance.

He doesn't respond. Instead, he takes another step, straight toward the gun.

"You don't wanna shoot me," he says.

God, I hate that he can see right through me.

"Answer me! Why are you here?" I growl, clenching the shotgun even tighter.

Before I know it, he's grabbed the barrel and points it

straight at his heart. "Go on then."

In a panic, I freeze. My finger almost pulls the trigger, but no matter how much I wish I could, I can't.

"Shoot me," he says.

I should. I really should.

But my finger refuses to budge.

I scramble to pull the barrel away, but he won't let go of it no matter how much I try to jerk it free. Instead, he yanks it out of my hands with sheer force and chucks it away out of my reach.

He's right in front of me now, blocking the way.

"See? You feel something."

"I *don't*," I hiss back, knowing I'm like a leaf trying to fight an unending storm. We're bound to clash, and I won't win this. He will. But I will go down as a liar before I admit that to anyone and *especially* him.

His face is rigid as always. "Stop lying to yourself, Lillian."

Just hearing my name come from his mouth makes the goose bumps appear all over my skin.

"Don't you dare," I say. "You have no right."

"I know," he says. "But I'm still here."

"How did you even do it?" I ask.

"I won't bother you with the details. Let's just say some guards can be easily persuaded." He shrugs. "I've done enough time."

Of course, he thinks that. As if he's the one to make that call.

"Tell me why you came here," I say, my voice sounding more desperate with every uttered word. "Why now, why here, why is it like this?"

He scratches the back of his head. "I needed to see you."

"Bullshit!" I spit. "Stop lying."

"It's the truth." His face shows no remorse, no change in emotion. It's as if he's convinced this is the way even though he knows it isn't right. None of this is.

"No!" I shove him away. "You don't get to say that. Fuck no."

"It's the only reason I'm here, I promise."

"How are you even here?" I ask, not sure I want to know.

"I have my ways." He shrugs.

"Of course, you do." I shake my head. His "friends" made it happen, of course. "Why should I expect any different? I don't even know you."

He makes a tsk sound and laughs it off as though it's no big deal. "You haven't changed at all."

"Really? Because I don't even recognize you," I snap back.

"You don't mean that," he says, cocking his head and smirking. "You're only saying that because you're angry with me. And you have every right."

"Yes, I do. You're not supposed to be here, and you know that."

"I don't follow rules well, Lillian," he says, still closing in on me. "But I'll listen to you. Tell me to leave."

I grate my teeth, trying to get the words across my lips, but no matter how hard I try, they won't come out.

"Say it."

I shake my head. I need these feelings to go away. I need to stop thinking about him in ways other than what he truly is … a stalker. I shouldn't even let him get close. "I can't."

I back away slowly into the house, shoving and pushing anything in my way aside. I almost trip over a pair of boots and a cabinet but manage to regain my balance just in time. He follows me inside, taking one step for every step I take.

"I want you. Both," he says.

"Shut up," I say, trying not to listen to his sinful voice that pulls me in with every word he speaks.

"No. I did that once. It got me nowhere," he says, clenching his fist.

Suddenly, I'm up against the closet door underneath the stairs, and he's already placed his hand against the wood. Unable to move and helpless to stop him, my only option is to stare him down and speak up.

"This isn't your home anymore."

"That's a cruel thing to say, Lil." He scoffs, his hand reaching higher and higher, as if he means to taunt me with danger. And it's working, all right, because sweat is dripping down my back.

"Don't be scared," he says, leaning in. "I won't hurt you. I could never."

That's hard to believe, coming from him. "How do I

know for sure?" I say through gritted teeth.

"Lil ..." He makes a face. "Really? You hurt me."

"No, *you* did. You made your choice." I push back again, rage filling my veins. "And stop calling me that."

"What, you don't like the nickname?"

"Nicknames are for good people. Not stalkers."

"Oh, I'm a stalker now?" he says, setting my soul on fire with the guttural laugh that escapes his throat. "All right. I guess you're right if that means I get to be close to you and—"

I smack him right in the face. "Don't you say her name."

It's quiet for some time.

I hope he got the point, but maybe that was a bit rough.

Then again, he's shown up on my property uninvited. I should've used the shotgun. Even if I couldn't shoot him in the heart, maybe I could've shot him in the leg. Or the arm. Or both. For good measures.

When he turns around to face me again with a clear red mark on his face, he leans in even closer, and whispers, "I'm sorry, Lil."

His words bring tears to my face. "Don't ..."

"I can't stay away. I just can't," he says, licking his lips as he places his other hand right beside me on the closet door, trapping me in his arms. "I want you. I need you. It's all I ever think about. All I want. It's the only thing in the world that I need ... you."

"No. Don't do this to me," I say, shaking my head, wishing it wasn't true that my heart almost jumped out of my chest hearing that.

I hate him. I *should* hate him with all my guts.

But I guess that's love …

It's unending, unyielding, undeniable. Even when the whole world feels like it's shifting on its axis and coming undone, love never ceases to exist.

So when he plants his lips on mine, I don't fight back. I don't push him away.

I let him kiss me … and overtake my soul.

FIVE

HANSON

Finally, she's mine, and I'm not letting go.

I grab her face with both hands and kiss her hard, letting her know how much I've missed her. I want her to feel it in her entire body. I want her to taste it on her tongue.

Fuck. I want her as much as I wanted to smell the fresh morning air while I was still in jail.

My skin itches with the desire to claim her. To touch her, lick her, fuck her.

God, how badly I wanna fuck her raw.

But first, I need her to know I'm here for her. That I'm not going to let her off the hook without at least a good memory to store for later because I'm definitely going to go to town on her.

As I start to lose myself in the taste of her lips, I'm unable to keep my hands to myself as they find their way down her pajama shirt. I wrap them around her body and pull her close, groaning into her mouth. The smooth curves underneath my coarse hands are a stark reminder of what I could've had all this time if I'd made a different choice.

But I didn't, and I don't regret it for one second.

I still get to have her, right here, right now.

So I kiss her even harder, deeper, pouring every ounce of myself into this one night we could have if she'll let me. If she'll have me.

"Wait," she mutters between ragged breaths. "It isn't right."

"Fuck right or wrong," I growl, planting another kiss right below her lips, and then another one on her neck. "I need to have you. I need to give you what you deserve."

Her lips shudder, and I can hear her breath more rapidly as my tongue trails all the way to her ear. I suck on her earlobe and moan into her ear.

"I've missed the sounds you make when I kiss you like this. I've missed the breaths you don't take when I touch you right here, Lil." I cup the small of her back with one hand and squeeze her ass with the other. "Mine."

***

Lillian

I tried to push him away, I honestly did. But the way his hands caress my skin and his lips merge so perfectly with mine make him impossible to ignore. Makes it impossible to deny these feelings bubbling up to the surface.

I wanna fight, but I can't ... I'm lost in his penetrating eyes, his all-consuming stare, and his tongue as it wraps firmly around mine. He claims me with his mouth like no one else ever could. But it's *him* ... the man I shouldn't want ever again.

"Hanson, I can't," I whisper, almost unable to separate my lips from his.

"Yes, you can. Just this night. Just one night," he says with a sultry voice. "That's all I want."

I need to stop this. Goddammit, Lillian, stop this!

"Yes."

The word slips off my tongue as easily as his kisses do.

Like poison injected straight into my veins.

I've never craved a man this much before in my life, but the moment his hands dive underneath my shirt, I instantly forgo all resistance I had. I can't stop it any longer, can't stop the need to surrender from rolling over me like a tidal wave.

His hands are all over me, touching me in places I

forgot I loved to be touched so much. He knows exactly where to caress me, slowly but roughly pulling me into his embrace. I'm still pinned between him and my closet, desperate for more as he plants kisses all over my neck and chest.

A second of air is all I get as he tears off his shirt and chucks it on the ground. The gaze in his eyes is murderous, like a lion that finally caught its wounded prey. And I am willing ... like a meek lamb, I let him take me over. He gropes my breasts, fondling my nipples until they're hard.

"Fuck me, have I missed these tits," he groans, while rubbing up against me.

He takes my nipple into his mouth and sucks hard while gently nibbling to keep me on my toes. I tilt my head back as he kisses me fervently, not giving me time to even respond. Right as I open my mouth, he latches on again. Sucking on my bottom lip, he coaxes my tongue to join in the game.

But this little voice inside my head keeps telling me to put a stop to it and make him leave. As our mouths unlock, I try to mumble, "Hanson, we—"

"Don't fight it, Lil," he groans into my mouth, and he captures my lips in another kiss.

I'm helpless to fight the desire. Helpless against the onslaught of emotions from seeing this man again. This man who stole my heart and kept it chained to his.

He grasps my waist and lifts me up against the door in his strong arms, still kissing me hard and fast. With a strong grip, he carries me toward the stairs. That's when I realize what's upstairs.

"We can't go upstairs. Daisy—"

"I don't need to go upstairs to fuck your brains out, Lillian," he says with a deep, resonating voice that brings chills to my bones. "I can do just that right here."

SIX

HANSON

I set her down on the staircase and rip off her pajama pants, throwing them into a corner. I'm not wasting any time now that she's finally let me in. Lucky for me, she wasn't wearing a bra, and now I find out she's not wearing any underpants either.

"What a surprise … no undies," I mutter, raising a brow.

It was as though she was expecting me.

A blush appears on her face, and it's the prettiest color I've seen in a long time.

"I always sleep like this," she says, cutting it short.

But she hasn't *always*.

I smirk as I grab her face, and say, "Relax, I'm not here to judge. I'm here to give you pleasure, so enjoy the ride."

With two fingers, I easily part her legs; they slide open as if she never even had the will to fight to begin with. I know it's hard to resist the pull when you've been dying for love for so long. The longing to be touched, to be licked … it can make or break a person.

Especially when they've gone so long without any. And she's definitely not had some for a long time … that I know for sure.

Cupping her ass, I bury my face between her legs and suck on her clit. Her eyes practically roll into the back of her head.

She tastes so damn delicious, and it makes my mouth water. I remember this taste and the way she gets all wet from the feel of my tongue circling her lips.

"Oh God," she whispers, and she grasps a handful of my hair, her fingers scrunching up as though she wants to tug. I wouldn't even mind.

"That good?" I murmur, grinning against her skin.

I go down on her hard, flicking my tongue and kissing her everywhere. I stick my tongue inside and circle around, letting her know how much I've wanted to do this. She moans in excitement, unable to contain herself even though her eyes tell me she wishes she could.

"Come for me, Lil. Let me see that beautiful face," I say as I lean up to take a peek.

She shakes her head while biting her lip. "She'll hear."

"She won't if you're quiet. And if you are, I can do it again, and again, and again …"

"Fuck," she hisses, curling her toes.

She's so fucking close I can taste it. When she comes, her mouth draws open, and the most delicious sigh escapes. Her clit grows under my tongue as I gorge myself on her. I push a finger inside to get a feel of how much she's enjoying herself as her muscles contract around my finger.

When her orgasm subsides, I lift her in my arms again. She almost squeals, but then captures her own voice inside her mouth. She hisses at me instead. "What are you doing?" she asks as I carry her up the stairs.

"Taking you in bed," I answer.

"You mean *to* bed."

"No, taking you"—a lopsided grin forms on my lips—"*in* the bed."

I slip upstairs as quietly as I can and open the door with my foot. I march inside and place her down on the bed and then immediately unbutton my pants. But then she replaces my hand with hers while I'm working on my zipper.

I pause and gaze at her, raising a brow.

She doesn't say a word. All she does is stare back at me while she sits on the edge of the bed with her hair undone. She looks beautiful. Picture perfect. And I can't help but run my hand through her hair to remind myself of what I've missed.

All these years.

It's been too long. Too long without a woman. Without

her.

When she's lowered my pants and boxers in one go, my dick springs loose. I was already hard from the moment I laid my eyes on her outside. It's only gotten thicker since we came upstairs.

She eyes me for a moment, biting her bottom lip. Then she grabs my shaft with both hands and starts massaging me, and fuck me, does it feel good.

I tilt my head back and enjoy her working me, rubbing me off like she wants me to come all over her. Maybe I will. Or maybe I want to savor this moment a little bit longer … because who knows how long it'll last.

Suddenly, something wet wraps around my length. I look down. It's her tongue, sucking me off. Jesus fucking Christ. And the way she does it makes me want to come instantly. But I hold off a little longer to enjoy her mouth.

I fight the urge to grasp her face and thrust inside. It's hard not to, but I have to remind myself she's not just a mouth but an actual person. Someone I care about. Someone I love so deeply it hurt not to be close to her.

And fuck me, do I want to be close to her right now.

I want to fuck her until dawn and beyond.

***

Lillian

He gently nudges me back until I stop sucking him and look up at him. The content look on his face gives me goose bumps. It feels so wrong but totally right at the same time.

He keeps pushing until I'm lying flat down on the bed, then he crawls on top of me. Time seems to be slowing down as he plants his lips on my skin. With my eyes shut, I let myself drift off into heaven, knowing full well the consequences of what we're doing.

He's a stalker.

A murderer.

And now an escaped convict too.

Nonetheless, I still want him.

Does that make me a criminal too? Probably. But there's no way I can say no either. Not to this man … God knows, I've tried. But I'm lying to myself if I said it wasn't my fault for letting my heart stay wide open for him to grasp. It's as if I personally invited him to come in and play.

And oh boy, can he play all right.

His tongue slides down my neck while his hands are all over my body, groping my breasts, my thighs, and even my pussy. He can't get enough of me, and the sheer feel of his body pressing down on mine is intoxicating.

My legs instinctively open as he rubs himself against me.

His tip brushes along my pussy, enticing me, pulling me in. I buck my hips, and the moment I do, he plunges in.

I gasp, and he covers my mouth with a deep, all-consuming kiss.

He thrusts into me with everything he has, slow but sensual, steady and merciless. Our kisses are frantic as our bodies seem to melt together, sweat drops mixing with passion. Balls deep, he buries himself inside me until everything I knew about myself disappears, and all that's left is pure need.

As his climax approaches, a grunt escapes his throat, and he pushes in deep. I can feel his cock tighten inside me. Then a warm jet filling me. I moan, satiated, feeling complete while ignoring all the warnings shouted by the little voice in my head.

It's too late for warnings. Too late for regret.

Because when I turn my head to take a breath, Daisy's right there … standing in the doorway.

SEVEN

Lillian

Shit. She saw us.

"Mommy?"

I scramble to grab the blanket and cover us up. But I'm sure she already saw more than she should have. "Hey, honey," I stammer, trying not to sound completely out of it. "What are you doing up? You should be sleeping."

"I couldn't sleep anymore. It was noisy." She rubs her eyes, and says, "What's going on?"

"Nothing, honey." I nudge Hanson to get off me and snatch a night robe off the floor next to my bed, slipping it on as I get out of bed.

She blinks a couple of times, staring at us. "But ... isn't that the man who gave me Mr. Puddlewuddle?"

I rub my lips together, wondering how I'm going to explain this. She saw me turn into an emotional wreck every time he came close to her. She saw me get mad and yell. I can't even imagine what's going through her head right now. She must be so confused. But I don't want to lie either.

"Yes, Daisy. That's him," I say, willing the blush on my face to go away.

"But I thought you said you didn't want me to talk to him? Now he's here in our house," she says, yawning.

Guilt eats me up as I grab her tiny hand and pull her out of the room, leaving him behind. "Mommy can explain, but let's get you some warm milk first."

I help her downstairs and into the kitchen where I settle her on a seat before I take the milk from the fridge to warm up in the microwave.

"So is he a stranger or not?" Daisy suddenly asks.

I pause. "He's your daddy."

"My daddy?" Her voice fluctuates in tone, and I know exactly why.

I told her she didn't have a daddy, but she did. Once.

I give her the mug and sit down with her. "I know I told you he was gone, but he wasn't gone forever ... just for a long time."

"Oh, so I *do* have a daddy?"

"Mmmhmm." I don't know what to say. He's a criminal. Not someone to look up to. How could she ever call him her daddy?

Hanson follows us downstairs in his pants, watching from the sidelines. He studies her closely but doesn't take another step.

"How come he never came to visit?"

"I couldn't." Hanson speaks up, but the moment he does, he immediately shuts his mouth again as if surprised by his own words. He takes a step back again and gazes at his feet, probably wondering if he should stay or go. If he's even welcome here.

"It's okay," I say, adding a soft smile. "You can come closer."

"You sure? I don't want to—"

"It's too late to take back what we did," I say.

He takes a deep breath and nods, then approaches.

"Hey, Daisy," he says as she watches him with a curious look on her face. "So I take it you liked the stuffed toy?"

"Love it," she says, revealing the plush from underneath her shirt. "He wants me to carry him with me."

"Oh, does he now?" Hanson smiles, and for some reason, it ignites a warmth inside my heart I didn't know I could feel.

Damn.

I'm falling hard when I really shouldn't.

There's so much wrong with everything that's happening right now, but what can I do? What's done is done, and I can't change the past. The only thing I can do is make sure the future is better. That her future is guaranteed to be okay. That she's happy. That's all that matters.

And I think he knows that too.

He places his hand over hers and squeezes softly. "I've missed you."

She smiles. "So you're really *my* daddy?"

I guess it's hard for her to believe, but he nods, laughing. She was too young to remember him, but now she'll probably never forget.

"But Mommy said you—"

"Mommy said a lot of things to protect you, sweetie," he interrupts. "And for good reasons."

"How come you were away for so long?" she asks, raising a brow.

"Daddy had to do something important," he says, cocking his head. "I'll tell you when you're older."

"Aw …"

"Daisy," I say, trying to distract her, "Do you remember the card? In the mailbox?"

Her eyes light up. "Oh! Can I read it?"

"Yes, go grab it!" I say, and she immediately pulls her hand out from underneath Hanson's and runs off to the mailbox just outside the door. I'm not afraid she'll run off with him here. She's way too curious.

Hanson breathes a sigh of relief. "I've missed *this*. Us. Together."

"Then maybe you shouldn't have—"

"I had no other choice!" he says harshly.

It's silent for a while until he clears his throat, and says,

"I apologize. I shouldn't have yelled."

I bite the inside of my cheek, unsure how to respond. He should know by now how I feel about all of this. That none of it should've ever happened. But here we are anyway, sitting in my kitchen and pretending we're not a completely fucked-up family.

"It's a card from Daddy!" Daisy says cheerfully as she runs back toward us, flailing the card around in her hands.

"And what does it say?" I ask.

"That he likes seeing me happy and that he wants to buy me more toys!" she says, and she makes the cutest squee sound ever. "Thank you!" She jumps up and down in front of Hanson.

"You're welcome, kid." He tousles her hair, making her giggle.

While she finishes her milk and keeps reading the card over and over again, it grows quiet.

"So what now?" I ask, gazing at him. "You know you can't stay."

He takes a deep breath. "I know. I just want you to know the truth."

A pang of guilt surges through me. I immediately get off my seat and grab Daisy's hand. "C'mon, time to go back to bed."

"But I don't wanna. I wanna stay with you guys," she protests, but she doesn't need to hear this.

I stop halfway to the staircase. "It's time for some grown-up talk, Daisy. You're not old enough yet."

"Aww but I wanna know too!" She crosses her arms and pouts.

I let out a breath and bend over to her level. "You will, one day. I promise. When you're older."

"Promise?" She gazes up at me with big bug eyes.

"Promise," I say, winking. Then I hug her tight and kiss her on the forehead. "Now, go on. Back to bed."

She nods and runs back up the stairs, and I stay to watch her close the door to her room as well before I return my attention toward Hanson.

Rubbing my lips, I casually saunter toward him and place my hand on the table. "The truth."

"Yes. I've wanted to explain everything to you for so long—"

"What's there to explain? You're a murderer, plain and simple." I grab the mug sitting on the table and bring it to the counter. I don't need to hear an explanation. Not for killing people. There is no reason. No way to talk this right. He left his family the moment he made that decision, and I cannot forgive him for that.

"He was a criminal, and you know that," Hanson says.

I almost smash the mug right there and then, but I manage to stop myself. Barely.

"That doesn't make it okay," I say, spinning on my heels so I can look him in the eyes. "You killed a man. Nothing he did makes that okay."

His face darkens. "Did you forget what he almost did to Daisy and countless other girls at the daycare?"

"Stop. I don't wanna hear it," I say, looking away. I'm already glad I found out in time to save my little girl. I can't imagine what she would've had to endure if the cops hadn't arrested that man when they did. And those poor other girls … God, I don't even wanna think about it.

"Ignoring it doesn't make it go away," Hanson says, pulling me from my thoughts.

"I haven't ignored it!" I slam my fist on the counter. I know I'm yelling. I just have to pray to God she can't hear me right now. "I've seen what it's done to the other girls and what it almost did to Daisy. I've lived with the consequences of choosing that fucking daycare. I know what I almost did to her." Tears fill my eyes. "What about you? Do you know?"

"I've done my best."

"So have I," I hiss back. "You. Weren't. Here."

I want him to know how much I hate him and how much it hurts.

Or at least how much I *want* to hate him.

"I wanted to be. More than anything," he says after a while.

"Then maybe you shouldn't have killed that guy," I say through gritted teeth. If it wasn't for him and his choice, none of this would've happened. Instead, I had to lie to my little girl about her daddy.

"I had no other choice," he says.

"There's always another choice," I spit back as rage bubbles to the surface.

"No." He takes a few steps toward me and makes a fist. "This was the *only* choice. You wanna know why? *Her*." He points at the stairs.

I shake my head. "Don't you bring her into this."

He moves in closer, right up to my face. "*She* is the reason. And I'd do it all over again if it had the same result."

"Why?" I ask, tears rolling down my cheeks.

He grabs my jawline with both hands and stares me down. "She's *alive*."

My lips part as I try to understand his words. Alive? What does he mean? "But—"

I suck in a breath, realizing what he means.

"I killed him to *save* her."

EIGHT

Lillian

His words resonate in my ears; their implication endless.

"What? But ... that's impossible—"

"How else do you think she survived?" he says through gritted teeth. "It was the *only* way."

I shake my head. "But you, you killed him ..."

"*For her*," he says.

I'm trying to fit the missing pieces together. That day, when I was at work ... when I heard on the news he was arrested ... that's when it happened.

"But how? I didn't even know—" I mutter.

"I didn't want you to know because I knew you couldn't

live with yourself if you knew how she survived," he explains. "So I told everyone to lie to you."

Tears keep rolling down my cheeks. It's too much to take in. Too much for my heart to accept.

Because if this is true, how can I stay mad at him?

"I'm sorry," he says, shattering everything I thought I knew about myself. About him. About us.

"I'm so sorry," he repeats. "But I made this choice, and I would do it again if I had to."

I do the only thing I can. I wrap my arms around his neck and kiss him. Deeply. Madly. Hard.

I'm lost in my emotions, lost in him, lost in my mind. Because I know none of this can stay the way it is. Everything changed the moment he made his decision, and now, after all these years, I finally understand why.

"Mommy?"

***

HANSON

Daisy's voice makes me pull back, and Lillian also takes a step back, pretending nothing was going on.

"Yes?" she mumbles, adjusting her robe and rubbing her lips together to hide the evidence.

"I forgot to say ... the noise that woke me up was a

car."

She frowns. "A car?"

This house is pretty much out in nowhere-land. Whoever comes along these roads is either visiting her or her neighbor. But who in the world would be traveling in the middle of the night? Except me, of course.

"Yeah," Daisy says. "I went to the window to look outside and see who it was, and I saw an old lady standing on the side of the road. Near the gate."

Lillian's eyes widen while I grab Daisy by the shoulders. "The farm's gate? What did the old lady look like?"

"Um ..." She touches her lip and looks at Lillian, who nods in agreement. "She had a yellow scarf, and her hair was up high."

Fuck.

This is definitely not good.

"That's my neighbor," Lillian says. "What's she doing here in the middle of the night?"

"What was she doing there?" I ask Daisy in a hurry.

"I don't know. I think she was on the phone," she says.

Fuck. Definitely fuck.

"That woman saw me in a shop downtown the other day," I explain, rising to my feet.

Lillian's face turns white as snow. "You mean ...?"

I nod.

She covers her mouth with her hand.

"She's calling the cops. Who knows how long she's been standing there."

"Shit but that means they'll be here any minute now," Lillian says, her voice unsteady.

She's right. "My car's on that road too." I run my fingers through my hair. I'm not worried. I knew this would happen eventually. It was only a matter of time.

"You can't leave," she says, shaking her head.

"I know. I'll stay," I say resolutely. "I've known this was the only outcome for a long time."

"What?" Her lips part. "But that means you intend to go back to prison? No. They'll put you away forever if they catch you."

"I deserve it," I say, licking my lips, thinking about the time I could've had with her. Thinking about all the kisses I've missed and all the touches we've had to forfeit. I don't regret it for a minute. Not even a chance. Because *she's* alive. Daisy lives.

So I grab Lillian's face and press my mouth to hers, claiming her one final time. I want her to know I won't leave her. At least not in the heart or mind. I'll be there every step of the way. "I love you," I say. "You'll never know how much this one night meant to me."

"No ..." She sucks on her bottom lip, barely able to keep it together. "Stop, please."

"You knew as well as I did that it couldn't stay this way forever," I say. It was a wish we both knew would never come true.

"This can't be happening," she says, hugging me tightly. "Not again."

"You know they'll never let me stay with you," I say.

"But I finally know why you did what you did. You saved her ... and now they'll take you away again? It's not fair!" she says, trying not to explode in rage in front of her little girl. "I'm sorry, I just ..."

"What's wrong, Mommy?" Daisy asks.

Her voice alone is enough to pull Lillian back down to earth. She smiles at her little girl, and says, "Nothing, Daisy. It's all right. We're just talking about our options here."

"There are no options," I say. "You and I both know that."

Lillian's face turns sour. "Don't say that. Not after dropping all that on me here. After all this time ..." She hiccups from the bomb I just dropped on her.

I can tell it's hard for her to grasp. For her to accept what's about to happen.

I grab her face again and make sure she looks me straight in the eyes. "I'm not going anywhere." I press my finger onto her heart. "I'll be there. Always."

"That's not enough," she whispers.

I feel the same way, but I know it's not going to happen. No matter how much we dream about it.

"It has to be enough. For our little girl," I say.

"She didn't make this choice, dammit!" Lillian paces around the kitchen, getting more agitated by the second. "Is she going to lose you again?"

Her words cut into me like a knife through butter.

"There's no other outcome to all of this. I knew that

when I escaped that prison, Lil," I say.

She keeps pacing around, ignoring everything I'm saying until she abruptly comes to a stop.

"There is," she says, not even looking at me while she utters the words.

My brows draw together. "What?"

When she gazes up at me, the look on her face has shifted to something more ominous. Like she's suddenly a whole different person, and it brings chills to my spine.

"Daisy ..." she says, approaching her. "You have to say goodbye now."

"Why? Is he leaving again?" she mumbles, rubbing her eyes.

"It's time for you to go to bed soon ..." Lillian says, smiling at her and running her fingers through her hair. "Mommy wants a hug and a kiss now."

Daisy wraps her little arms tightly around Lillian's body. It gives me goose bumps to watch the intense bond these two have. It also reminds me of what I've missed all these years.

When they're done hugging, she says, "Go to the back of the house. Don't go outside. Just wait there."

"Why?" she asks.

"You'll understand soon," she says, smiling as the tears well up in her eyes again, but she swallows them away. She presses another kiss to Daisy's cheek and pats her on her back. "Go on."

When Daisy's left the room, I grab Lillian's shoulder,

and say, "What are you doing?"

"Making a choice," Lillian says, giving me a bitter smile.

Like we're saying goodbye when we're not supposed to.

It's all happening so fast. I wish I could put a stop to it, but I know just as well as she does that this could never be.

Right then, sirens in the distance are heard.

They're here.

"Quick. You gotta leave," she says.

So quickly did she change her mind about me. Not that I'm complaining. I'm grateful that she wants to help me out, but ...

"I'll never get outside fast enough," I say, shaking my head.

"Yes, you will. Here, take this." She shivers as she grabs a coat off the hanger and wraps it around me, along with a scarf and a hat.

"My car is out front. No way I can get there in time before the cops get here."

"You can take my truck," she says.

My eyes widen, and I realize what she's about to do. "No, Lil."

"Yes," she says, pushing me to the back of the house.

"You can't do this," I say.

"Yes, I can." Not only has her voice changed, but her whole attitude has done a full one-eighty. "I'm not letting them take you away. Not when she finally has *you* again. Not when I finally know why you did it."

She can't stop the tears from flowing anymore, and even

I am tearing up as I hold her hand and squeeze.

"Take her," she says. "I want her to grow up safe and sound ... with you."

"But I'm a criminal—"

"I don't care!" she says, wrapping her arms around my neck. "She needs you like I needed you."

"She needs her mommy," whisper into her ear.

"You know what they'll do to her if they find me here with her. They'll put her in a foster home. You didn't sacrifice everything to have her go there, and you know that," she says, looking me directly in the eyes.

"Then stay here and let me—"

"No. You've done enough," she says. "It's time I took the burden," she says with a heavy voice. She grabs a box and pushes it into my hand. "This contains all her medicine. Make sure she takes it every day. You can get more at the pharmacy. She's got a prescription. She visits the doctor every month. Make sure she gets checked regularly." She swallows. "Oh, and she hates blueberry pie, but loves blueberries on pancakes."

I smile and nod, gazing into the bag. There's a bunch of bottles filled with pills.

It looks like there's no point in fighting her. This is how she's always been. Stubborn to the bone. Just like her little girl. Just like me.

"I'm doing this. Don't think of convincing me otherwise," she adds.

"All right." I sigh. "You'll be aiding and abetting a

criminal. You know that, right?" I say with a dead serious face.

She nods, her stance unchanging, her voice resolute. "I'm aware."

I hug her tight. "Thank you."

"No. Thank you," she says. "For finally trusting me and releasing me from the pain."

It feels like ages before we can finally let go of each other, but the sound of the police getting closer and closer forces us to. But I refuse to release her hand. I smile at her, and it's the toughest smile I've smiled in years.

"Take care of yourself," she says.

"I will."

"And make sure she stays innocent. I don't want her to know," she adds.

I nod. Understandable. "I will."

When we finally release each other, compelled by the sirens, I move to the back of the house while she stays and watches me pick up Daisy. One final glance is all I need to know she's a hundred percent sure of what we're about to do.

So I open the door, and I don't look back as I run with Daisy.

NINE

Lillian

When the police arrive, I walk out onto my porch and meet them head-on. Two vehicles pull into my driveway, turning off the sirens when they step out their vehicles. They immediately walk toward me, hands firmly on their holsters.

"I was just about to go to bed. What's going on?" I ask, yawning.

"Ma'am, we got reports that a fugitive has been spotted at your house," one of them says, eyeing my house.

"There's no one here except me," I say.

I'm not lying. There is actually no one else but me.

"Your neighbor alerted us to the black Volvo outside your home. Is it yours?"

"No," I say, shrugging. "I have no idea who it belongs to."

That *is* a lie, but they don't have to know. And if they do, it doesn't even matter anymore.

Daisy and Hanson are already long gone by now. They drove off in my truck about fifteen minutes ago, and I have no idea which direction they went. And the police probably let them drive right past them because they were looking for a black car, not a green truck.

"Ma'am, we'd like to search the premise, please," the man says.

It's not actually a question, more like a statement, and I get it. They don't trust me. They have every reason not to.

The man they're looking for was … *is* still my husband.

And I know they were expecting him to come here.

They just didn't expect him to take weeks to finally make that decision.

And they probably, no definitely, didn't expect me to let him run off with our daughter.

But they don't know me, and I didn't know the full story to my husband's killing.

Now that I do, I don't intend to ever doubt him again. He might be a murderer, but because of him, Daisy is still breathing. How could I ever stay mad? Without him, I wouldn't have even gotten the time that I now had with her.

As the police officers search the house and realize he's

not here, they ask me the same questions again, still clutching their guns. "Ma'am, I'm going to ask you again. Did Hanson Locklear show up at your property? Is he here?"

"No," I say. It isn't a lie. He isn't here … anymore.

The police officer narrows his eyes at me. "His car is right outside your gate."

"Is it?" I raise a brow, pretending to be surprised as fuck.

He glances at the shotgun on the ground, and says, "So you pulled that out for nothing then?"

"Maybe." I shrug. "I heard some noise last night. Went to check, but it was nothing."

"Nothing? Hmm …" he murmurs, looking down at his boots while muffling a laugh. "Interesting."

One of the policemen walks out of my house, holding up a piece of clothing that belongs to Hanson. His boxer shorts, more specifically. Guess he jumped into his pants in a hurry and left them here.

"Well, would you look at that? Didi's Garments from town," the police officer says as he looks at the label inside the boxer shorts. "Oddly specific and they look brand new. Maybe we should ask the owner who bought these."

The other police officer keeps his eyes fixated on me. "Ma'am, I didn't spot your truck outside. Where did you park it?"

"Maybe the barn. Maybe the village. I don't remember. I usually walk home," I lie, licking my lips. I don't even care anymore.

"Right." He puts his hands against his side.

"Are we done here?" I ask with a straight face.

I know they can see right through my bluff, but I don't mind. I'm not telling them a damn thing. I'd rather go down lying than lose my dignity.

"Yes, ma'am." The police officer rummages in his pocket and takes out a set of shackles. "I think you know as well as I do that you're hiding something. You're coming to the station with us. Now, are you going to come without making a fuss, or do we have to restrain you?"

I hold up my hands, and say, "That won't be necessary."

I knew this was coming. Even if they couldn't identify who bought the boxer shorts, it'd be pretty easy to find out who has my truck, considering Hanson left his own car right in front of my house. One plus one equals two.

I don't look back as they escort me to the police car. I'm sure I'll be charged with aiding a criminal, so I probably won't be back here again. At least not for a long while.

I won't miss this house. Hell, I won't even miss my freedom.

The only things I already miss are them … my little girl and my man.

All I can say is that I'm grateful. Grateful for the time we got together, grateful for the man who will now spend the rest of his time with her, and grateful that our love transcends even the worst of circumstances.

I will go down with my head held high before I will ever

let them find my husband and our little girl.

They deserve to be together, and he deserves his freedom. He's suffered enough.

And if that means I'll have to serve time … so be it.

I'd willingly hang for both of them.

***

HANSON

From a distance, I watch as they drive into the parking lot of the police station. She's in there. I could probably grab her and run, but knowing her, she wouldn't even come with me.

She'd hold onto the metal frame of the car for dear life.

Not because she wants to go to jail, but because she knows this is the only way for Daisy to grow up safe and sound. Because that's what we both want most of all.

Even though she's now left with a man she barely knows. A fugitive. But I won't let them get their hands on her. She won't go into the system. Not on my watch.

Instead, I'll raise her somewhere far off in Mexico. Somewhere no one will take her away from me. Where we can live out our days in peace.

Lillian would've wanted me to.

I can tell from the look in her eyes. No regret. Nothing

but steadfast perseverance.

Just like me.

I guess it's to be expected with her finally knowing why I did what I did.

Maybe I should've told her sooner.

But who would ever say to their wife *Hey, I killed a man to save our little girl?*

No one.

Except me.

TEN

HANSON

Before

I grab the dead man's body and drag it onto the bed, then cover it with sheets. I rummage through my bag and put on the nurse's outfit and a fake badge, prepping for what's to come. I grab his health chart and check it, making sure everything's still the same as it was the last time I snuck into the hospital. I already know everything I need to know, and this chart confirms that. How ironic is it that he's the one; the perfect match.

I put my hands under a running faucet and run my fingers through my hair, then I put on some fake glasses. A quick glance in the mirror is all I need to confirm that it's spot-on. It's go-time.

Without hesitating, I grab the bed and wheel it toward the door. Before I pass through it, I take one last deep breath, knowing it could very well be my last.

I peek around the corner. The guard keeping an eye on him has gone to grab his lunch. Perfect timing.

I roll the bed into the elevator and take it up to ward fifteen. I pass several nurses and doctors and greet them with a smile. They're busy talking about their work today. None of them seems to notice the fact that my patient is out cold. Or rather … dead as a doornail.

Good. They'll notice me soon enough. But not until I'm where I want to be.

I roll the bed into the ward and find the room I'm looking for. I'm glad no one has tried to stop me. I don't think they would've survived it if they did.

I wheel the bed beside the little girl, lying in the other bed and hooked on the machines.

Seeing her still robs me of my breath and shakes me to my very core.

My little girl.

Liver failure, they said. She wouldn't survive.

I begged them to take mine, but I wasn't a match, and neither was her mommy.

Her body has given up, but her willpower hasn't. I'm sure of it.

Time is running out. They'll be here soon, and I have to be prepared. I take off the nurse's outfit and grab my bag. I take out a bomb vest and tie it to my chest. No need to cover up anymore. When someone sees me, they'll know exactly what I want.

I load another gun and tuck it into my pocket. Then I sit on Daisy's bed and wait. I grab her hand and hold it tight, pressing a soft kiss to her forehead. "It won't be long now. You'll be with Mommy soon."

She doesn't answer, of course. She's in a coma right now and unresponsive. But I know she's in there somewhere.

Though I wouldn't want her to see me like this, wouldn't want her to remember her daddy like this. As a criminal. A murderer.

I swallow away the lump in my throat as I realize there's no way back. This is it. This is when it's all going down. And the moment a nurse steps into the room, I get up and point my gun at her.

Her eyes widen, and she freezes, bewildered. She almost screams, but I place a finger against my lips, and say, "Don't."

Her chest rises and falls. She's panicking, I can tell, so I have to act as quick as I can.

"Contact the OR. Tell them to get ready," I bark.

"Why?" she asks, her voice shaky.

"She's getting the operation. Today," I say. When she doesn't move, I yell, "Do it!"

She immediately grabs her phone and calls the staff. I don't know exactly what she's saying, but I'm pretty sure she's including the fact she's being held hostage and forced to make a call. But I don't care. Let them know how badly I want this, and how much I'm willing to sacrifice.

When all is said and done, more staff enter the room. I guess they got the call too. But none of them move beyond where the nurse is, probably scared of getting shot. However, I'm outnumbered now, and that increases the risks I'm not willing to take, so I show them my bomb vest.

They take a step back in fear, some of them picking up their phones again, probably to call the police. I don't give a damn. I already knew they'd be coming anyway. Right now, all I care about is my little girl.

"Is the OR ready?" I growl.

"Yes, but why? What do you plan on doing?" the doctor asks. "She's just a little girl. You can't—"

"She's my daughter! Goddammit. Don't you people understand?"

My desperate plea comes across as they all grow silent, their faces turning white.

"There's a body there," I say, pointing at the bed. "Bring it to the OR too."

"Okay …" the nurses say. "But the OR is for—"

"Do what I say, and no one gets hurt," I bark, showing them the bomb vest again so they know I mean business.

One of them swallows and steps forward, clutching the bed. "Okay. Let's take her to the OR then."

More step forward, trying to wheel her out, but I won't take my hands off the bed.

"I'm coming with you. I'm not leaving her side," I say.

They all look at each other and nod, but I can see the disapproval in their eyes.

It doesn't matter if they think this is right or wrong. I need to be there so I know things get done.

"Roll them both to the OR," I command.

It's going slow, but everyone is finally moving, doing exactly what I say while keeping my little girl alive. They wouldn't want to jeopardize a living, breathing person. That's not what they signed up for. They made an oath, and now I'll force them to keep it.

So we all roll out into the hallway. There's tape everywhere, and an alarm is going off. All the staff have left the area except the ones accompanying me. Behind the tape, police officers are screaming at me.

"Put down your weapon. No one has to get hurt," one of them shouts.

"And I don't intend to hurt anyone as long as everyone does what I say," I shout back, then turn toward the staff. "Now go to the OR."

"What is it that you want?" the surgeon asks.

"For my little girl to live," I say.

"All right. We can make that happen," he says, holding up his hand. "Just put down the weapon and kick it over here."

I frown. "No … We're going to the OR."

I know they're trying to negotiate with me, trying to make me release the "hostages." But that's just it. I don't care about them or myself. I just want my little girl to be okay. What happens after that doesn't interest me.

So I force everyone to move into the elevator and down to the OR. Even there, the police are waiting, but no one stops me from going inside. Of course not … they're terrified I might detonate the bomb around my waist.

I won't as long as everyone does precisely what I want them to do.

"Prepare the room like you normally would," I say, pointing at the staff to get to work.

When they finally move, one of them, a woman, approaches me, and says, "But what are we supposed to do?"

"You're going to operate on her. Give her a new liver."

The woman's eyes widen. "But there's no transplant available."

"Yes, there is." I march toward the other bed and rip off the blanket, revealing the dead guy. "Here."

They're all glaring at the dead body now with faces pale as snow.

"But we can't do that. He might not be a match—"

I point my gun at the one who's talking so they all know I mean business. "I've done my research. He's a perfect match. She can survive on pills, can't she?" When they don't answer, I repeat it much louder this time. "Can't she?"

Some of them nod, and others look on in dismay. They're probably wondering if I'm serious.

I am dead serious.

I don't give a damn how they do it, but they are going to

give her his liver, and they are going to make it work. No fucking question.

"You give her that new liver. She. Lives. That's my only demand." As they wait for my next move, I flick the gun, and say, "Now get to work."

"But you have to put on a gown first," one of them says with a shaky voice. "To keep everything sterile." When I stare her down, she adds, "You don't want her to get sick, do you?"

"Fine." I nod. When she hands me the gown, I put it on with a bit of trouble because I want to keep my gun where they can see it. After I place the mask over my mouth, they all carefully scrub in themselves and begin.

I stay put while they do their thing. The bed is prepared, and my little girl is placed on top, still hooked to the machines. The anesthesiologist makes sure she's under and won't feel anything. One surgeon makes the incision in the dead man's body and prepares the donor liver while another surgeon cuts my little girl open. The nurses and doctors all take utmost care for her and the transplant, but I can tell they're on edge.

I don't blame them. It can't be easy to do your job when there's a man with a bomb vest pointing a gun at your head. But I can't let them go either. Not until it's done.

It feels like it takes ages for them to give her the transplant, but I don't move a muscle until they're finished.

As they sew her back up, I ask, "Did it work?"

"Well, we've cut out the cancerous parts, but her body

took quite a hit," the surgeon explains, taking off his bloody gloves.

"Tell me the truth," I say, trying not to look at the wound in my daughter's belly. It hurts to watch, but I have to keep looking to make sure it's done correctly. If it helps her live, then it's a necessary evil.

"So far, her body is accepting the liver, but we don't know for sure until—"

"Will she survive?" I interrupt.

"If she takes her meds …" the doctor says. "Probably, yes."

The nurses attempt to wheel her bed away, so I stop them. "Where are you going with her?"

"The recovery room. She needs to come to from the anesthetics," the nurse explains.

"Her body has been through a lot," the doctor says. "She needs time to heal."

"How do I know you won't take the transplant out when I'm gone?" I spit, not taking any chances.

The doctor raises his hands. "We never take out transplants unless they're being rejected."

"So if her body accepts the liver, she gets to keep it?"

He sighs out loud then, and with a bleak face, he says, "Yes."

I breathe out a sigh of relief too. "And the body? What will you do with it?"

"The coroner will handle it."

I nod a couple of times. "One final thing … don't tell

my wife. Ever. I don't want her to know where Daisy got her transplant. Got it?"

"But she needs to know her girl is going to get better," the doctor says, frowning.

I grab him by the collar. "She can't know the liver came from him, or she'll demand it to be taken out. I won't have it."

The doctor raises his hands, saying, "Okay. Okay. We won't say anything."

"Good." I walk toward the bed and kiss my little girl on the cheeks. "Stay strong. Get better fast. You'll be home before you know it." I squeeze her hand again. It's probably the last time I'll see her. Maybe forever.

I forfeited the right to regret my actions the moment I made this decision.

And as the nurses wheel her out, the doctors evacuate the OR, and the police come in to arrest me. I take off the bomb vest and chuck it away, then I go to my knees.

I won't fight. There's no reason to. Not anymore.

The police hurl me to the ground like wrestlers, sitting on top of me to restrain me and take my gun away from me.

I don't care. None of it matters as long as she lives.

I've fulfilled my purpose.

I killed a man and sacrificed my freedom to save a girl.

Anyone would do the same for their baby.

ELEVEN

Lillian

After

I stare at the picture of my daughter hanging on the wall. She's holding a blue balloon and a giant teddy bear with some tubes still going into her nostril. I took that picture when she was still in the hospital and kept it in my wallet to remind myself of how far she's come.

This photograph was one of the few things I was allowed to keep here in prison. It's all I need to keep me sane. To keep me going.

I'm fighting the system, but I'll do it the right way. My trial is coming soon, and my lawyers are doing their best to get me out. But until then, I'll stay put and wait out my time.

It was my choice to make, my decision that brought me here, and I don't regret it. Not even for a second.

Hanson finally gets to spend time with his little girl. The time he fought so hard to deserve.

If I'd known he'd killed a man to give Daisy a new liver, I would've asked the doctors to take it out even though I knew her chances were slim. She was not at the top of the list to receive one, and no donors were in sight. But my moral code would've stopped me from ever accepting what he did if I'd known he was going to do it.

No wonder he didn't tell me until now. He probably forced the staff to keep it a secret from me too, so I wouldn't ruin it. Of course, that's just like him. Always thinking ahead.

He sacrificed everything he had, and what did I do? I chastised him. Wished him dead for killing a man who was already going to jail and leaving his little girl without a father to grow up with.

And all this time, he only did it to save her.

To get her out of that hospital bed and back into my arms.

How could I not do the same for him?

***

HANSON

After

We stop at Dirk's Diner just across the Mexican border from Texas. It's far enough from any law enforcement that I feel safe enough to take a quick breather outside.

I don't think they know where we are anyway. I saw my face on the news when I was passing through, but I haven't seen any cops around for miles, so I don't think anyone called them on me either.

It's like no one cares around here, which is good. Gives me enough time to decide where I'm going to take Daisy. Where we're going to settle down. Maybe I should visit some friends down in Mexico City. They might have a job for me so I can provide for her. A safe job—not the kind that gets you killed but the hardworking kind. I'm not risking my life over money. Daisy needs to grow up with her daddy ... somewhere where she'll feel at home.

Daisy was scared of me at first. She wasn't screaming, but she was definitely crying when we got into her mom's truck. I felt bad, but it needed to be done, so I explained to her that we were going on vacation for a bit, and her mom would join us soon.

What else was I supposed to say? At least this made her less fearful at the time.

And now that we've gotten a chance to bond, we've

become best buds.

Speaking of, I still need to hand her the letter. The moment she saw her name on the envelope, it was over. She's been asking about it the entire drive here, wanting to know how and where I got it, and when she's allowed to read it. I explained her auntie hid them away and that a friend of mine picked them up for me, but she kept asking for more, so I had to stop explaining halfway through. She's too young to understand anyway.

"Daddy, can I see the letter now?" she asks as I take off my seat belt.

I sigh and glance at her over my shoulder. "All right, all right." I rummage in my bag and take it out.

"Who is it from?" she asks as I hand it to her.

"Your momma." I wink.

She makes an o-shape with her mouth and then jumps up and down, almost tearing the envelope. "Yay!"

She tries to open it with her little hands, but it takes her so long she gets frustrated and hands it to me. I swiftly tear it open and hand it back. "There you go."

"Thank you!" She pulls out the paper and reads the letter, taking her time to pronounce each word.

Dear Daisy,

You'll probably never read this letter, but I want you to know that at least I tried. I've told your auntie Dana to hold on to the letters I send her until I get the chance to hand them to you myself. As much as I want to, I can't be with you right now. But I promise it won't be long. I'll be with you soon again, before you even know it.

I know you'll be good. I know you'll do great out there in the world.

And you know ... I will find you again.

Love,
Mommy

When she's done reading out loud, there are tears in her eyes, but she wipes them away with swift hands.

"I wanna see her," she mumbles.

It breaks my heart to hear her say that, but what can I do? This is the choice Lillian made. The choice we both made when we decided to value Daisy's life over our own. I still don't regret making that choice, and I promised myself I never would, for her sake.

But she doesn't need to know any of that. I won't ever tell her how she survived. I want her to grow up without fear, without feeling judged for someone else's actions. I want her to be young ... innocent.

And if that means not letting her see her mom, then so be it. Bringing a kid this young to jail would definitely scar her, not to mention the fact that they'd arrest me on sight. That's the last thing either of us wants to happen.

So I sigh, and say, "We can't, at least not right now." I

grab her hand and squeeze. "But you'll see her again real soon, I promise."

"Will Mommy come to our new house too?" she asks.

"Someday, honey, when she's ready," I say, rubbing her head. "But first ... who wants some pancakes?"

She throws her hand high up in the air, her face lighting up like a million light bulbs. "Me, Daddy, me!"

I do love it when she calls me daddy.

It makes me feel like less of a criminal ... and more of a man.

EPILOGUE

Lillian

My sentence was completed after four months of jail time. The judge thought it was a long enough time for me to realize that I shouldn't aid criminals, but he realized my situation was unique too, so he didn't want to give me too hard of a time.

Smelling the fresh air again does wonders for one's soul.

Plus, the idea that I'm out of that hole and free as a bird puts a smile on my face. I finally get to see my little girl again.

I wonder how she's doing. If she's missed me as much as I missed her.

If Hanson took good care of her while I was gone.

I grin. Knowing him, he gave her all the cuddles in the world.

The last time I saw him was when we separated and said goodbye. He didn't come to my trial, but he had a good reason. I, on the other hand, did not. I couldn't stomach seeing him after knowing he killed a man. And I didn't want to put my baby girl through seeing her father in shackles either.

When he called me to tell me he was in jail, I hung up and never spoke to him again. I completely withdrew from him and everything surrounding him, including his proceedings, because it was too much to handle. After all, my little girl had miraculously survived after receiving a liver from an organ donor. She was in recovery. That was more important to me.

Maybe I should've gone to him or the authorities to demand an explanation for what he did. It would've made it easier for me to understand his actions. But I guess he knew me better than I know myself.

I stare out the bus window, getting more anxious the closer I get to the street they're living on. I got the address via his friend Brandon, who contacted me right after I got out of jail. Apparently, once Hanson left the country, it was impossible for them to arrest him, so he could freely tout his location without getting caught.

The bus makes the final stop, and I grasp my bags and jump out. It's only a few blocks farther. The neighborhood isn't perfect, but it looks safe enough with lots of working-class houses and families walking around.

As I approach the right house, a little girl comes storming out the door.

I guess she saw me from the kitchen window.

"Daisy!" I yell as I drop my bags and open my arms until she runs right into them. I hug her tight, and whisper, "God, I've missed you so much."

"Mommy! You're home."

Home.

I smile. I like that word.

And I like it even more the moment he walks out and shows his face.

We're a family once again.

***

HANSON

The wilderness beyond Mexico City isn't like it was back at home, but at least I can enjoy it in freedom. The sand whips up each time the wind blows, and we struggle not to close our eyes. Still, we all can't help but smile at each other as we sit in front of the fire on the small camping ground we've made. A family reunion vacation, sort of speak.

For me, it's a time to say goodbye to my old life in jail

and to the sins of my past. To welcome a new life for all of us. So I sing the only song I can think of, the only song that makes sense; the song my people once sang.

Ahala Ahalágó naashá gha, (I am going in freedom,)
Shí naashá gha, shí naashá gha, (I am going in beauty all around me.)
Shí naashá lago hózǫ́ǫ́lá.
Shí naashá gha, shí naashá gha, (I am going, I am going, in beauty;)
Shí naashá, ládéé hózǫ́ǫ́lá. (It is around me.)

The one song that always makes my daughter smile.
God, I would hang for that smile.

The End

###

THE HANGED MAN is just one of the many stories in the Cards of Love Collection. Which card will you choose next?
www.cardsofloveromance.com

Read on for an excerpt of CAGED!

EXCERPT OF CAGED

PROLOGUE

CAGE

My thumb brushes over the reflecting image of a girl with hair so white it could blind a man like me. Licking my lips, I stare at her delicate shape in the white dress, her soft posture as she leans into the green trees around her, and the way she wistfully stares at the blue sphere above her head. One moment is all it takes to capture her beauty. And I know I'll have a lifetime to discover it.

I smile, cocking my head. "Her."

That's all it takes. That one word … and she becomes mine.

I can't stop staring at her eyes. Those soul-crushing blue eyes seem so pure. So vulnerable. Unlike me.

But when the image is snatched out of my hands, my smile immediately dissipates. I turn my head and watch him take the pictures down from the glass, one by one, until nothing's left but a gray stone mass behind it. No life. No green. No blue. No nothing.

I sigh out loud.

A hand touches my shoulder, squeezing. "Don't worry … You'll see more than just a picture soon."

The hand disappears, and I'm left alone again in my cold, dark space.

But one thing has changed.

Me.

ONE

Ella

The scent of freshly baked bread enters my nose and fills me with joy. I point at the loaf I want and smile.

"That one?" the baker asks.

I nod, and he grabs it from the shelf and wraps it in paper then puts it on the counter. I already have the money ready to pay, so I place it next to the loaf. He swipes it off and stuffs it into the cash register.

"Thank you very much," he says. "Enjoy!"

I smile again while picking up the loaf and tucking it into my bag. Waving, I leave the store and face the sunlight again. I love how the warmth radiates over my skin, how it makes me want to close my eyes and take a deep breath. Summer is the time I come alive.

On my way back home, I take a detour through the park and pick up all the flowers I like. Red, pink, yellow—as many of the crazy colors as I can gather. Their aromas waft through the air with every summery breeze, and I love to just take it all in. Like a moment frozen in time, where everything is exactly the way it should be.

Untouched.

Perfect.

Unlike me.

***

Twelve Years Ago

I pick up two rocks and stuff one into Suzie's hand. "You go first."

"No. Why do I have to go first? You know I'm not good at this," she whines, putting out a pouty lip. "Why can't we just do it my way?"

"Because we already did that yesterday. Now, we do it *my* way," I say, frowning. "Now c'mon. Throw it."

She sighs, so I rub her back. "You can do this. Just throw it like this." I bend my arm and chuck the stone at the pond, and it skips across the water like a bug until it sinks.

"Wow, that's far!" Suzie yells, her face full of amazement. "But wait ... I was supposed to go first, right?"

I shrug. "We weren't playing for real yet. But now we are. C'mon. Throw the stone."

Her face lifts with a smile. "Okay, I'll try."

I nod a few times, which only makes her smile bigger. I cheer her on. "Go!"

She aims and then throws as hard as she can, but the stone immediately sinks to the bottom just a few feet from where we stand.

"Aw ..." she mumbles with chagrin.

I clap my hands. "My turn."

I snatch another stone from the ground and do it just as I did before, and it pitter-patters across the water farther than Suzie's stone did.

She puts her hands on her side. "Fine, you won."

"Yay!" I jump up and down. "I get to be the princess now."

"But we do it *my* way tomorrow," she says, grimacing. "Rock, paper, scissors."

"But that's just boring," I reply.

"No, it's not!" she quips. "I do it all the time with Bobby. He says it's much better too."

"I don't care about Bobby. Bobby's a boy; I'm your sister. Big difference."

"So?"

"So I get to say what's much better. And this is much better." I pick up another rock and hold it out to her. "If you want to get better, I can teach you."

"Really?" she asks, taking it and tucking it into her

pocket.

"Yeah, of course. That's what sisters are for, right?" I grin, and she hugs me. "All right. Now, let's play," I say, wrenching away from her arms.

As I run for the tree, Suzie chases after me, and I glance over my shoulder and giggle. "You won't catch me!"

"Yes, I will!"

"No!" I pat the tree just before she does. "I win!"

"Fine," she snaps as I climb up the shoddy ladder to the makeshift treehouse. It's just a bunch of wooden planks stuffed between the trunk and some curtains hanging from the branches, but it's my house now.

"Here!" I say as I pick up the clothes I brought here from home and throw them down to her. "Put this on!"

"Why?"

"Because you're the prince, of course," I say with a cocky face. "Why else?"

She rolls her eyes but does it anyway while I put on the pink dress I brought. Mom doesn't exactly know I took them from the dress-up box, but she won't notice. I'll bring them home without a scratch, and if they have smudges, I'll wash them out myself. I'm a big girl.

I pat down my dress and twirl. It looks so pretty.

"Ready yet?" I yell down as I wait for my prince to come rescue me.

Except when I peer over the edge of the treehouse, no one's there.

Suzie's gone.

"Suzie?" I yell.

It's quiet. Too quiet.

I wonder where she went.

I step to the other side of the treehouse and look down there. She's standing near the road just a few steps away from the trees ... and she's talking with a man.

A man I've never seen before.

A tall ... no, a big guy with a beard and scary looking scars. His face is dark as he speaks to my sister.

I wonder what they're saying. I think it's something I should hear too.

I try to listen to their conversation from where I'm at up high, but I can barely hear anything. Except for a couple of words ...

"Will you be my friend?" the stranger asks.

"Sure," Suzie says.

She keeps talking to him even though Mommy told us not to talk to strangers. Did she forget? Or doesn't she care? Either way, I'm worried, so I start climbing down the ladder.

"Ella?" It's Suzie, and she sounds like she's in trouble.

"Who is that?" I yell, but she doesn't respond, and I can't see her anymore as the trees block my view.

But I can clearly hear her scream.

***

I immediately jump down the last few steps and run to her. The man has grabbed her hand and is dragging her to a car.

"Ella!" she screams as he pushes her inside and closes the door.

"No!" I scream, my lungs barely able to handle the force of my voice.

The man gets into the car, and before I can get to her, he drives off.

Within a second, I've grabbed my bike and jumped on it to race after them. I don't care that I'm wearing a pink dress or that I'm crying my eyes out. I have to get to her. I promised Mom I'd look after her. I promised Mom I'd take her back home. I have to.

I have to bring Ella home.

The car's right in front of me, but I can't seem to catch up, no matter how hard I push the pedals of my bike. I'm out of breath, out of energy, but I won't give up. However, the longer it takes, the more I'm left behind.

I can't keep up.

The car disappears, but I keep going. Keep biking. I'll go on forever if I have to. Because I have to get her back. I'll get Suzie back. No matter the cost.

It's almost sundown, and I'm supposed to be home by now, but I can't go back. Not without my sister. My mom would kill me. I promised. I promised.

Tears run down my cheeks as I follow the only road the car could've gone.

And then out of nowhere, it appears.

My heart skips a beat, and a hopeful burst of energy

makes me bike harder to get to the car. Parked on the side of the road, it's near the forest my mom told me not to go near because it was way too big and we could get lost.

But getting my sister back is more important than rules.

So I dump the bike between the fallen leaves on the ground and make a run for it. Through the woods, I follow the trail. Tracks in the earth and leaves show me where they went. It can't be far.

The salty tears on my face have dried up, and determination has taken their place. I keep going and going without knowing where I am, but as long as I find Suzie, I'll be okay. We'll be okay.

Thick branches push me back, but I don't stop wading through the darkness of the forest. I don't stop for anything. Not for the pain I feel in my legs. Not for the monsters that could lurk in the dark.

Except for a cliff ... right in front of my feet.

I barely manage to stop in time before I fall.

That's when I see it.

A body lying down there on the cold, muddy ground. Hair tangled with twigs, face bloodied and twisted.

It's Suzie.

I scream, but the sound disappears into a sea of trees echoing my voice.

"I'm sorry."

A voice makes me turn my head toward the direction its coming from, just behind a tree not far from Suzie.

"I only wanted someone to talk to," he adds.

It's him. The man who took Suzie.

He quickly turns and runs, disappearing into the forest.

Without thinking, I slide down the slope of the cliff, careful not to fall as I rush to her. I wrap my arms around her and shake her, but she doesn't respond.

"Suzie?" I call out her name maybe three, four ... fifteen times.

Nothing I say or do reaches her.

No matter how many times I push her, how many tears roll down my cheeks, how many times I scream—nothing will bring her back.

The more I cry, the less my voice is heard. And even though I try, the sound of my voice keeps fading until nothing's left.

Nothing.

Suzie's gone and so has my voice.

She screamed my name, and I didn't get to her in time. She lost her voice because I refused to use mine. And now it's all gone.

She's *gone*.

But I promised Mommy ... I *promised*.

And now I'll never bring her back home.

TWO

Ella

Present

When I've gathered enough flowers, I stroll through the streets until I get to the cemetery. I open the iron-clad fence, its loud squeak a stark difference from the silence up ahead. As I walk along the pebble path, I notice I'm not alone, but that's okay. Everyone here has lost someone dear to them, and not a single soul would dare to say they don't miss them.

I do too.

I place my hand on top of the cold stone in front of the grave and say a prayer. Sometimes, I even talk to her in my head.

I brought you these flowers.

I place them on the grave.

I know you always loved to steal them from the park, so I thought I'd pick them for you instead of buying a bouquet. Are you okay here? Do they treat you well in the afterlife? I hope you don't miss me too much. I promise I won't be long. But I won't come until it's my time. I know you'd want me to enjoy the life I have here. It's just hard, you know? Of course, you know ... you lived it.

I sigh and bite my lip.

Twelve long years. And still, nothing has changed.

The world still revolves around the sun. People live their lives, oblivious to the pain of others. And me? I'm still stuck in that same memory ... still unable to move on.

I turn around and make my way out of the cemetery, determined not to stick around for too long or else I might even spend the day. I have to get this out of my head. Have to find my happy place again.

Turning the corner, I start across the bridge over the river and stop in the middle. I grab my loaf of bread and pull off a few pieces, chucking them into the water. The ducks and seagulls quickly gather to gobble them down, fighting over every last bit as if it's the only food they've gotten in a week. Except they're as fat as can be, so that can't be it. They're so used to people that they practically follow me around just to get more of that bread, and it makes me giggle. Especially when one of the ducks nibbles on my dress.

I try to shoo it away but have no luck. When I twist and spin on my heels, I notice a car with tinted windows on the road at the end of the bridge. A man in the driver's seat has rolled his window down and is staring at me.

A chill runs down my spine.

I don't know why, but when he drives off seconds later, I feel like I can finally breathe again.

To this day, every single incident scares me. Makes me want to scream with the voice I've lost long ago.

I'll do anything to stop the terror, so I start walking. Even with all the ducks chasing me, I keep going. One of the ducks latches onto my dress again. I pull it back and throw another piece of bread behind me. They're so busy and distracted that I can make a run for it.

I'm completely out of breath when I get home. I can't believe I got so worked up again over just a car. It was fun feeding the animals, though.

I take off my coat and put the loaf away then I put a cup of water in the microwave and heat it up. After I make a cup of hot tea, I sit down on the couch and pick up my Kindle. I love reading … and I love tea. It's odd because most people I know don't drink tea, but I love it. Then again, I'm not like most people.

I like silence. I like the serenity it brings. Silence is when the world is still spinning, and everything is okay. Silence is what I'm used to. It's all I've known since …

I choke up just thinking about it.

I gaze at the clock and at the pictures on my bookcase.

They're so unique and detailed. I can't stop looking at them from time to time. I made them myself. Dad always says it's okay to be proud of yourself even if it's a small thing.

I smile to myself, thinking of how happy he was when I picked up this hobby, as he calls it.

To me, it's my job. I sell these pictures to newspapers and magazines—whoever is willing to pay for them. They're my bread and butter. I can live off it, so it's more than just a hobby. Even though it doesn't make me rich, it's something I can do. Something that doesn't require me to talk to people. Something that makes me feel less out of this world.

Sipping my tea, I enjoy the day until it's time to cook. However, just as I'm about to get up, I hear the lock in my front door rattle. Seconds later, Bobby, or Bo as he likes to call himself nowadays, bursts in with a paper bag filled with groceries.

"Hi, Ella!" He's always so vibrant; it amazes me.

I wave.

"Feeling good today?"

I nod.

"Sorry about the sudden entry. I just thought I'd surprise you by cooking for you. That okay?"

Bo's sweet; I have to give him that even though he just barged into my home.

He does that from time to time—to check up on me, I suppose.

Ever since my sister's gone, he's been keeping an eye on me. It's like he feels responsible for me, in a way, which is cute.

"I've got some fresh veggies here that we can cut up," he says, placing the paper bag on the counter.

He didn't have to buy all that, but I can't say no to a hearty meal either, especially when he cooks it. His dishes taste much better than mine do.

"Mac and cheese but with veggies?" he asks, turning around to wink at me.

I nod, smiling.

"I knew you'd be a sucker for it." He points at me and laughs. "One mac and cheese coming right up."

He's too sweet for his own good. Always taking care of everyone. I don't remember him being any different, at least not toward me.

Other people sometimes say he's a weirdo because he's so shy and doesn't have many friends. But I don't mind. I'm the same, so I guess that makes us friends by default.

I smile to myself, watching him toil about in my kitchen. He's such a kind soul, despite being so closed off to the outside world. He hides his pain and sorrow underneath thick layers of fake happiness. Anyone can see that. But I won't judge him for it. After all, I have baggage of my own to deal with.

When the food is done, we gobble it down together while watching television. Then we wash the dishes and play a board game. He doesn't talk much, but I like it that way. We both like the silence.

I just enjoy the time I have with him without feeling

judged. When we're hanging out, we focus on the good things in life. And it makes me happy … if only for a moment.

A few hours later, the day has already passed, and Bo has gone back home.

In bed, I lie awake and stare at the ceiling, wondering if my simple life will ever be anything other than boring. If I could ever handle anything else again.

Because as I turn in my bed and curl up into that comfy position, I still feel my heart banging out of my chest. The crippling fear that has chased me for so long still holds me in a vise grip every single day of my life.

And there's no way to escape.

No other way … but sleep.

***

I wake up to something covering my face. A sickly sweet smell enters my nostrils as I breathe, but it makes me want to vomit. My eyes burst open.

A man is standing mere inches away from me.

His hand covers my face. A damp cloth between us.

My eyes dart around the room, looking for an object I can use to smash his face in, but he's holding me down with his other hand. I'm paralyzed from both my fear and his control. And the more I struggle, the harder it becomes to breathe.

To move.

To see.

I'm weak—so weak and tired—but I don't want to close my eyes.

What is he doing to me? Who is he? Why is he here? How did he get in?

I want to open my mouth and scream, but when I do, nothing comes out.

His voice is all I hear … whispering to me like a snake right before I fade away.

"Shhh, it'll all be over soon."

***

When I come to again, the first thing I feel is a roaring headache. My lungs burn when I breathe through my mouth. A metallic taste lies on my tongue, and I swallow to make it go away, but it lingers. Everything hurts. My head. My mouth. As if I've been hit a couple of times, but I can't remember a thing.

And when I open my eyes, I'm still so dizzy; I can barely make out a thing.

It's dark as night. Not a single light surrounds me except the one at the far end of the room.

The room … with no windows.

No plants.

No sunlight.

Nothing.

All I can see is a gray concrete wall surrounding me.

I try to get up, but my feet don't feel like they belong to me, and I struggle to get anywhere. But I don't give up. I keep crawling across the floor, hoping to make it to the light, just so I can see where I am.

But I can't.

Not because my muscles gave up.

But because I physically, literally can't.

Between me and the light ... is glass.

I turn around, trying to find a way around it, but there's no crack. Not a single one in all the glass surrounding me. Not even at the top as I try to stand on my toes. Nothing ... but glass.

A cage.

My heart stops beating.

The panic rises again, bubbling to the surface.

I open my mouth and scream, but no sound comes out except for a faint sigh.

Just like always. My voice was taken from me a long time ago. And I know no matter how hard I try that no one will hear me.

Where am I? Who was that man? Where did he bring me and why?

With my back against the glass panes, I sink to the floor.

I can still barely make out my environment or feel my own skin. I'm numb from the drug he gave me and numb from the shock.

But I still don't cry. I close my mouth and stop breathing. I stop moving. Like a rock, I stay put and pretend

I'm not there.

Why?

Because something across the room, not far from me, still captures my attention.

Something lurking in the dark behind the glass.

I'm not alone.

CAGED – Available now!

THANK YOU FOR READING!

Thank you so much for reading Cards Of Love: The Hanged Man. I hope you enjoyed the story!

For updates about upcoming books, please visit my website, www.clarissawild.com or sign up for my newsletter here: www.bit.ly/clarissanewsletter.

I'd love to talk to you! You can find me on Facebook: www.facebook.com/ClarissaWildAuthor, make sure to click LIKE. You can also join the Fan Club: www.facebook.com/groups/FanClubClarissaWild/ and talk with other readers!

Enjoyed this book? You could really help out by leaving a review on Amazon and Goodreads. Thank you!

ALSO BY CLARISSA WILD

Dark Romance
Delirious Series

Killer & Stalker

Mr. X

Twenty-One

Ultimate Sin

VIKTOR

Indecent Games Series

FATHER

Caged, Locked, Chased & Branded (Coming late 2018!)

New Adult Romance
Fierce Series

Blissful Series

Ruin

Erotic Romance
The Billionaire's Bet Series

Enflamed Series

Unprofessional Bad Boys Series

Hotel O

Visit Clarissa Wild's website for current titles.

www.clarissawild.com

ABOUT THE AUTHOR

Clarissa Wild is a New York Times & USA Today Bestselling author of Dark Romance and Contemporary Romance novels. She is an avid reader and writer of swoony stories about dangerous men and feisty women. Her other loves include her hilarious husband, her cutie pie son, her two crazy but cute dogs, and her ninja cat that sometimes thinks he's a dog too. In her free time, she enjoys watching all sorts of movies, playing video games, reading tons of books, and cooking her favorite meals

Want to be informed of new releases and special offers? Sign up for Clarissa Wild's newsletter on her website www.clarissawild.com.

Visit Clarissa Wild on Amazon for current titles.

Printed in Great Britain
by Amazon